For my greenfingered mother,

~ with love ~

First published in the United Kingdom in 2003 by The Chicken House,
2 Palmer Street, Frome, Somerset, UK, BA11 1DS

Email: *chickenhouse@doublecluck.com*

Designed by Ania Mochlinska and Elizabeth B. Parisi

Reinforced Binding for Library Use
Library of Congress Catologing-in-Publication Data available

ISBN 0-439-40435-5

10 9 8 7 6 5 4 3   04 05 06 07

Printed in Singapore

First American edition, March 2003

Secret in the Garden

A Peek-Through Book

Inspired by Frances Hodgson Burnett's *The Secret Garden*

Written and illustrated by James Mayhew

The Chicken House

SCHOLASTIC INC.

New York

It was a hot, sunny day, and Sophie was all alone making
daisy chains. She had been reading her favorite book
about a girl and a secret garden, and now she was feeling
bored and sleepy. If only she had a friend to play with!
    Beside her was a high brick wall.
    "Perhaps that wall is hiding an old garden — a magical,
secret sort of garden," she thought.

As her head drooped, she saw, out of the corner of her eye, something glimmering in the trees.

What could it be?

It was a robin carrying a key in its beak! He swooped down and dropped the key into Sophie's hands.

"Where did this key come from?" she asked. "Somebody will be looking for this!"

The robin cocked his head as though he were trying to tell her something. Then he flew over to the wall. Sophie followed, holding the key. And there, hidden behind the ivy, was a door with a window!

Standing on tiptoe, Sophie peeked through and saw something hiding in the garden beyond.

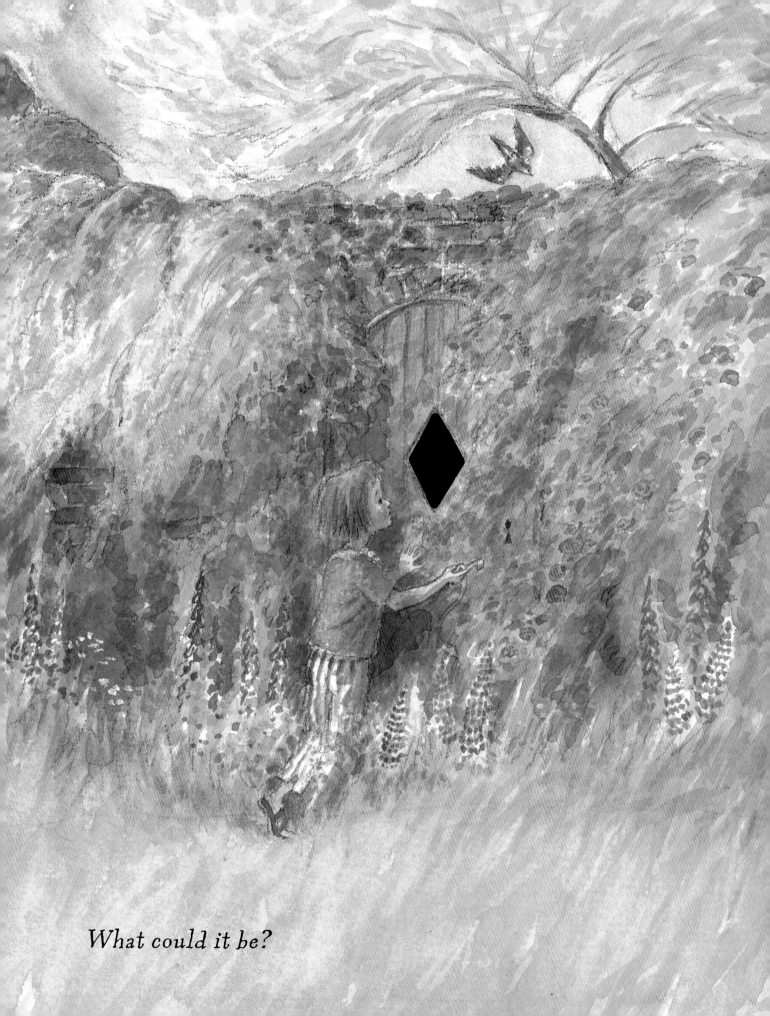

What could it be?

It was a little squirrel . . . playing with a hat!
"That hat's too big for you!" Sophie said, giggling.
"Somebody will be looking for this!"

Sophie put on the hat and set off to explore.
The robin led the way and the squirrel
scurried along beside her. Soon they came
upon a greenhouse with a broken pane
of glass.

Sophie was curious, so she peeked
inside and saw something hiding
in the corner.

What could it be?

It was a furry fox cub . . . playing with a doll! "What are you doing? Foxes don't play with dolls!" Sophie gently scolded. "Somebody will be looking for this!"

As she made her way through the garden,
Sophie felt sure that there was someone waiting
for her around each corner.

With the hat on her head and the doll
under her arm, she called for the squirrel and
the cub and followed the robin down the path.
Soon they came to a rose garden.

Sophie peeked through the thorny bush and saw
something hiding among the rosebuds.

What could it be?

It was a sweet, white lamb . . . tugging at a jump rope!
"Can you jump rope? I wish I could! But I'm sure it
doesn't belong to you!" Sophie said laughing. "Somebody
will be looking for this!"

Suddenly, a high-pitched whistle filled the air, and the fox cub scampered off into an orchard.

He looked around to see that Sophie, the squirrel, and the lamb were following.

Sophie peeked up into one of the trees and saw someone hiding in the branches.

Who could it be?

It was a young girl . . . smiling down at her!

The two girls looked at each other and Sophie said, "I'm Sophie, and I've found all of your friends and your things. And now I've found you!"

As she climbed down, the girl replied, "I'm Mary, and I've
been waiting for you to find me for a long, long time."
So Sophie and Mary, the robin, the squirrel, the fox, and the lamb
played in the garden. And Mary taught Sophie how to jump rope!

Later, the two tired friends settled down, and Sophie taught Mary how to make daisy chains. As the evening shadows began to fall, Sophie's head drooped and soon she was fast asleep in the tree.

The sound of someone calling her name woke Sophie with a jump.

Who could it be?

It was Sophie's mother.

"Have you been asleep?" she asked gently.

"I'm not sure," said Sophie. "But I've had a wonderful time making friends and finding a magical place to play, and at last I can jump rope!"

"But who taught you, and who gave you the jump rope?"

"Mary, my new friend," said Sophie.

In the Secret Garden!

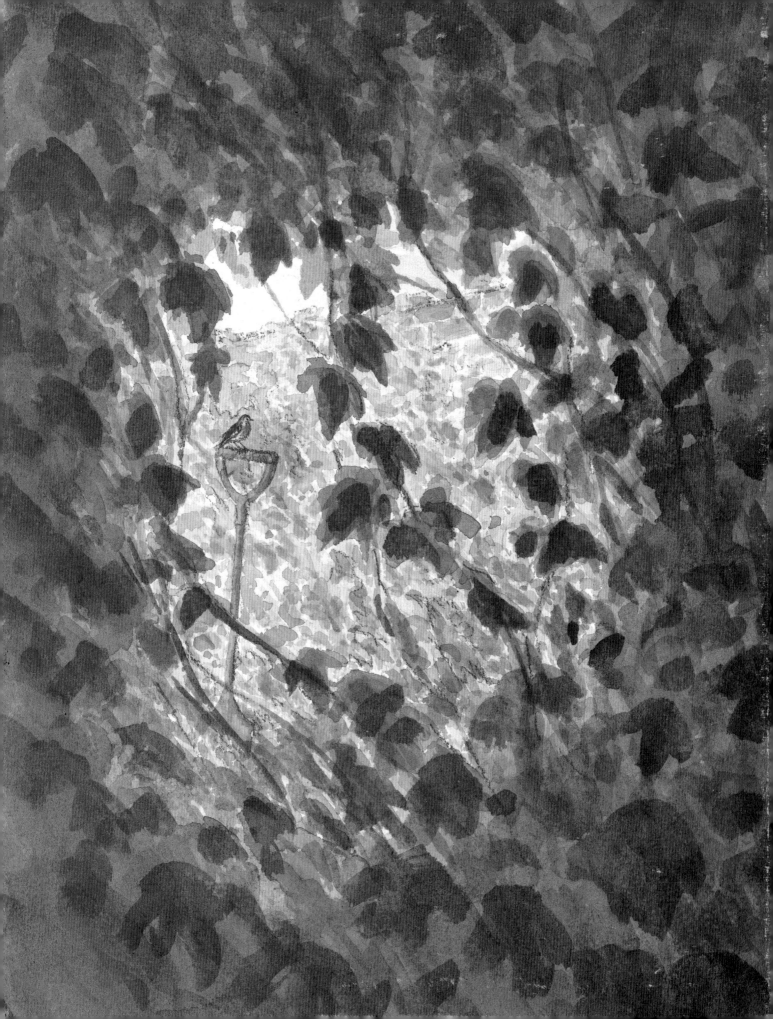